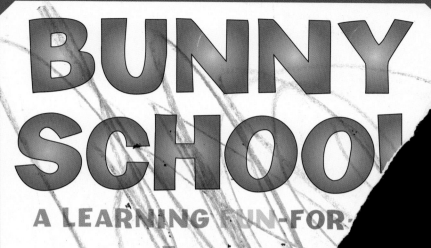

BUNNY
SCHOOL

A LEARNING FUN-FOR-

By **Rick Walt**

Illustrated by **Paige**

HarperColl

Show-and-tell, bunnies: Share what you brought.

Lovely rocks. An apricot!

That is a beautiful piece of string.

Oh, how fun! What an interesting . . . thing.

Good morning!
Today is _____.
The weather is _____.
This is _____'s
    special day.

Learning time, bunnies: ABCs,
Shapes and colors and 123s.
How many building blocks look the same?
Show me the way you write your name.

Music time, bunnies! Let's all sing.
Feel that rhythm: Pluck on a string,
Pound on a drum, bang on a gong.
We could make music all day long!

Recess, bunnies: Run for the slide,
Hop on a swing and take a ride.
Tag, you're it! Throw me the ball.
Here, I'll help so you don't fall.

Snack time, bunnies: First wash up.
Cookies on a napkin, milk in a cup,
Apples and carrots, all on a tray.
Remember to throw your trash away.

Science time, bunnies: Come and explore
Experiments from ceiling to floor.
Fill cups with soil, then in seeds go.
We'll water them and watch them grow.

Field trip, bunnies: In your neighborhood.
The doctor says you're looking good.
"Open!" says the dentist. The chef says, "Eat!"
See the mail carrier, and police on their beat.

Up next, bunnies: A firehouse tour.
Trucks and hoses and ladders and more.
Say hello to the firefighting team.
Turn on the siren and hear it scream!

Art time, bunnies: Paper and glue.

Here are some crayons and paints for you.

A boat, a car, a moon, a star . . .

Oh, what wonderful artists you are!

Playtime, bunnies! Find a friend,
Get a game out, let's pretend.
Puppets to play with, puzzles to do.
That tower is as tall as you!

Clean up, bunnies: It's fun to play,
But time to put our toys away.
Puppets on pegs, blocks in the bin,
Here's the box that game goes in.

Story time, bunnies! Take a look.
I'm going to show you a brand-new book!
Listen to the story carefully,
Then you can read this book to me!

School's out, bunnies! We had a good day.

But now it's time to go on our way.

Pack up your papers, everyone.

See you tomorrow when we'll have more fun!

To Rob and Nikki Ivie,
and their smart bunnies
Matthew, Nathan I.,
Nathan B., Russell,
Benjamin, and Erin.
—R.W.

To the children,
teachers, and staff
of Simon Lake
Elementary School.
—P.M.

Bunny School: A Learning Fun-for-All
Text copyright © 2005 by Rick Walton   Illustrations copyright © 2005 by Paige Miglio
Manufactured in China by South China Printing Company Ltd. All rights reserved. No part of this book may be used or reproduced in any manner whatsoever without written permission except in the case of brief quotations embodied in critical articles and reviews. For information address HarperCollins Children's Books, a division of HarperCollins Publishers, 1350 Avenue of the Americas, New York, NY 10019. www.harperchildrens.com
Library of Congress Cataloging-in-Publication Data   Walton, Rick. Bunny school: a learning free-for-all / by Rick Walton ; illustrated by Paige Miglio.— 1st ed.
p   cm.   Summary: Young rabbits spend a fun day at school, from saying hello to friends to packing up for tomorrow.   ISBN 0-06-057508-5 — ISBN 0-06-057509-3
(lib. bdg.)   [1. Schools—Fiction. 2. Rabbits—Fiction. 3. Stories in rhyme.] I. Miglio, Paige, ill. II. Title.   PZ8.3.W199 Sch 2005   2004000179   [E]—dc22
Typography by Carla Weise   1 2 3 4 5 6 7 8 9 10   ❖   First Edition